Published in the United States by ON Words Publishing, LLC.

For additional copies contact the publisher:

ON Words Publishing, LLC.
8720 Ferguson Ave
Savannah, GA 31406
www.onwordspublishing.com

Second U.S. Edition, June 2007

ISBN 0-9787589-2-9

Printed by Regal Printing Limited

Contact the illustrator at www.amiejacobsen.com

ON Words Publishing, LLC. will donate a portion of the proceeds from the sale of this book to organizations that support programs for children.

To the real Olivia and Noah who inspired
us to write this book.
~M.N. and R. N.

To Jared and Jessie, who scampered through Savannah with me!
~A.J.

"Hey kids," said Dad excitedly, "We're here in Savannah, the oldest city in the state of Georgia."

Savannah is a seaport town on the Georgia coast. Huge ships come up the Savannah River from all over the world.

"Let's get settled into our hotel and rest up," said Mom, "so we can prowl around and check out this cool, old city."

"Hey Noah," whispered Olivia, "I'm not sleepy, are you?"

"No. Let's go outside and check things out. I saw a really big oak tree outside the hotel that we can climb," said Noah.

"Wow Olivia, look at the view from up here."

"Hey Noah, look over there at that awesome pirate flag."

"Where?"

"Over there, let's climb down and go see it. Maybe there are real pirates and we can find some treasures."

"Cool, look at me Olivia!"

"Get down from there, you may fall and get hurt," scolded Olivia. "Let's go inside. They might have pirate swords, and hats and even some real gold coins."

"Wow, they do have cool pirate stuff in here,"
exclaimed Noah.

"This place looks really, really old. I bet real pirates used to come
here a long time ago."

"Hey, look at those girls going up the street. I wonder why they are wearing
those uniforms?" asked Olivia. "They have a bunch of badges on their vests too. Let's
follow them and see where they are going."

"They went in there, the Juliette Gordon Low House," Olivia said as she pointed toward the building. "Juliette Gordon Low was the founder of the Girl Scouts and this building was her birthplace. No wonder those girls are dressed in uniforms. They must be girl scouts."

"Look!" Noah said excitedly. "They have boxes of cookies. Let's get a box to eat, I'm starved."

"Great idea!" Olivia said. "There is a bench over there in the park we passed. We can sit down and take a break and have a snack."

"Hey, we are in Chippewa Square,"
read Olivia. "The statue is of General James E. Oglethorpe. He sailed across the ocean in a large ship over 250 years ago. He helped design the layout of the streets and squares in Savannah, making it one of America's first planned cities."

"These cookies sure taste good," Noah said to Olivia. "You know, Momma always said that life is like a box of cookies."

"Don't be silly Noah, that was from a movie, and I think it was a box of chocolates anyway."

"Hey little dudes, what's up?" asked the skateboarder.

"Well, we need to head back to the hotel where our parents are staying. The hotel is near the river where you can see the big ships. Do you know which way we should go?" asked Olivia. "Sure dudes," he answered.

"Sounds like you need to get down to Tybee Island. I'm headed that way now. Hop on the back of my skateboard and hold on tight!"

"Wee!"

"Hop off here little dudes. Climb up to the top of the lighthouse and see if you can spot your hotel. Good luck!" yelled the skateboarder as he zoomed off down the street.

"Thanks for the ride!" shouted Olivia and Noah.

"Wow, look at that lighthouse. It is taller than the trees. It almost touches the clouds. Let's climb to the top," begged Noah.

"Okay, but you can go first," Olivia said nervously.

"Did you know that the Tybee Island Lighthouse is the oldest and tallest in the state of Georgia?" asked Olivia.

"You can see everything from up here!" Noah exclaimed.

"Everything except our hotel," moaned Olivia.

"But look over there at that awesome fort and all those huge, old cannons. Let's go check it out!" Noah said as he headed back down the lighthouse steps.

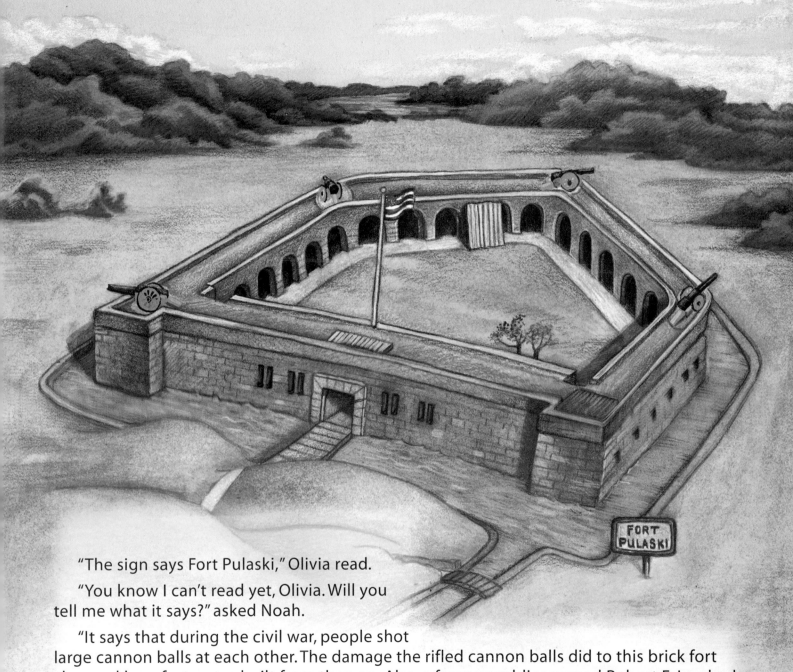

FORT
PULASKI

"The sign says Fort Pulaski," Olivia read.

"You know I can't read yet, Olivia. Will you tell me what it says?" asked Noah.

"It says that during the civil war, people shot large cannon balls at each other. The damage the rifled cannon balls did to this brick fort changed how forts were built from then on. Also, a famous soldier named Robert E. Lee had his first post at this fort."

"Cool! Look Olivia, there is a soldier over there. Maybe he can help us find our hotel."

"Excuse me sir, can you tell us where we can find the hotels near the big ships?" asked Noah.

"Big ships, huh" said the soldier. "Oh! I bet your hotel is in town near the Ships of the Sea Museum. Hop on that trolley right over there and catch a ride back to your hotel."

"Thanks!" called Olivia and Noah as they ran to catch the trolley.

"Attention passengers," a voice said over the loud speaker. "Our next stop will be the Roundhouse Railroad Museum. It is part of the oldest and most complete pre-civil war railroad manufacturing facility still in use. You can see steam engines, locomotives, model railroads and a lot more, so everyone off the trolley."

"Noah, look at that huge horse and that fancy old carriage."

"Who cares?" said Noah. "I want to check out all the awesome trains!"

"Well, I'm going for a carriage ride," Olivia said. "Maybe it will take us back to our hotel."

"Well okay," Noah agreed. " I am getting hungry, so we better head back."

"Do you smell that, Noah?" Olivia said as she sniffed in the air.

"I sure do. It smells like some really good southern cookin'," Noah said. "And the smell is coming from that restaurant. Let's go!"

"This is delicious!" Olivia mumbled with a mouth full of macaroni and cheese.

"Yeah. This is the best fried chicken I have ever tasted," said Noah. "I wish Mom cooked like this at home. Maybe we can get her a cookbook with these recipes before we leave town."

"Great idea!" agreed Olivia.

"Look Olivia! There is that big oak tree we climbed by our hotel."

"Let's hurry," Olivia said. "We better get back to our room before Mom and Dad wake up and start to worry about us."

"Great kids, I'm glad you're awake," their mother said. "It's time for us to get going. There are so many neat places around Savannah that we want to visit. I hope you are rested up!"

Olivia and Noah looked at each other and smiled.

The Lady's Cheesy Mac

4 cups cooked elbow macaroni, drained (approximately 2 cups uncooked)

2 cups grated Cheddar cheese

3 eggs, beaten

1/2 cup sour cream

4 tablespoons (1/2 stick) butter, cut into pieces

1/2 teaspoon salt

1 cup milk, or equivalent in evaporated milk

Preheat oven to 350 degrees. After macaroni has been boiled and drained, add Cheddar cheese while macaroni is still hot. Combine remaining ingredients and add to macaroni mixture. Pour into casserole dish and bake for 30 to 45 minutes. Top with additional cheese, if desired.

Random House, Inc.